THE GRAND
INQUISITOR

FYODOR DOSTOEVSKY

THE GRAND INQUISITOR

Introduction by
ANNE FREMANTLE

A Frederick Ungar Book
CONTINUUM • NEW YORK

2001

The Continuum Publishing Company
370 Lexington Avenue
New York, NY 10017

Printed in the United States of America

Library of Congress Catalog Card Number: 56-7503

ISBN 0-8044-6125-2

INTRODUCTION

FYODOR MICHAELOVITCH DOSTOEVSKY was born on 30 October 1821. He was the second son of a doctor, who had been an army surgeon until the end of the war of 1812, when he was appointed resident physician to the Marie Hospital for the Poor, where he lived with his wife and children, of whom there were eventually seven. The doctor was an aristocrat, his wife a *bourgeoise*; both were devout churchgoers; and they carefully supervised their children's education. The mother and children used to spend their summers in the country on a little estate the father had bought; here Fyodor got to know the peasants and became attached to the "blessed earth." He also read voraciously, the novels of Walter Scott and of Fenimore Cooper being his favorite books.

In 1837 Fyodor's mother died, and his father took him and his elder brother Mikhail to St. Petersburg, to board them there in the Government School of Engineers. But when the boys were medically examined, it was found that the robust looking Mikhail was tubercular; it was the delicate Fyodor who was passed as fit. So Mikhail went to the Engineers School in Reval, whose health requirements were not as high as St. Petersburg's, and Fyodor was left alone, and lonely, at the St. Petersburg school. He remained there three years, and in 1841, graduated with honors as an ensign. In 1843 he became a sublieutenant in the army.

Meanwhile his father, miserly, greedy, and corrupt, refused Fyodor an allowance, and his last letter to him was a denial of a small sum begged by Fyodor to buy a little sugar and tea to take on summer maneuvers. Shortly after, the father was murdered by his own serfs. The police authorities made little attempt to find and prosecute the actual murderer. "We cannot arrest a whole village," they said, "and the whole village is guilty." It was a communal crime, and even those not actually involved in it sympathized with the murderers. Among these was Fyodor himself, who, however, had his first epileptic fit on learning of his father's death. In all his novels, Dostoevsky emphasizes the collective nature of all crime. And all his books are about crime: "The guilt of every individual is binding upon us all, just as his salvation saves us all. Crime is the center of Dostoevsky's tragic world," wrote Romano Guardini.

Dostoevsky came to Moscow when he had finished with his military service; and one evening, after he had been reading aloud from Nicolai Gogol's *Dead Souls* (such readings were the fashion then), he gave the manuscript of his first novel, *Poor Folk*, to D. V. Grigorevitch, who read it then and there, and was so impressed that he took it to his friend Edward Nekranoff, an editor. Nekranoff was equally excited, and the two men walked round to Dostoevsky's house at four a.m. and rang his doorbell. "No matter if he is asleep," they said to one another, "we will wake him up. This is above sleep."

With the publication of *Poor Folk* in 1846, Dostoevsky found he had become famous overnight, and instantly he became part of a circle of writers and intellectuals as gifted, brilliant, and closely knit as ever existed anywhere. Although Dostoevsky was not a revolutionary (indeed, his friends thought him rather reactionary), yet he was arrested on 23 April 1849, and accused of complicity in a conspiracy, merely because, at a meeting, he had read aloud a letter from a notorious atheist to Gogol. Dostoevsky was condemned to death and spent eight months in the fortress of Peter and Paul. During this time he wrote *The Little Hero*. Then he was taken out, by order of Tsar Nicholas I, with twenty-three others. "They snapped swords over our heads, and made us put on the white shirts worn by persons condemned to death. Thereupon we were bound in threes to stakes, to suffer execution," Dostoevsky wrote to his brother Mikhail; "being the third in the row, I concluded that I had only a few minutes of life before me." But instead of the expected shot, the troops "beat a tattoo," and the men were reprieved, though one had gone out of his mind under the ordeal. Dostoevsky was sentenced to four years hard labor, in chains, in Siberia, and to a further six years of exile from Moscow as a private in a Siberian regiment, under strict discipline. Only in 1859 was he allowed to return to Russia. Yet he always refused to condemn his judges: "It was just," he said. "The people themselves would have condemned us."

On his return to Moscow he started a magazine, *Vremya*, which was suppressed by the censor; and a second, which he founded later, *Epoch*, fared no better. While in Siberia, he had married a friend's widow; she and his brother Mikhail both died in 1864, and Dostoevsky took on his brother's debts, although terribly burdened by his own. In 1867 he married again, and had four children. He published *Letters from a Dead House* in 1861-2; *Crime and Punishment* and *The Idiot* in 1866; The *Possessed* in 1871; and *The Brothers Karamazov* in 1880. His youngest son, Alyosha, died at the age of three, of epilepsy, a disease inherited from him. So the circle of guilt was complete: Dostoevsky felt implicated in both the death of his father and of his child. After the boy's death, Dostoevsky went to the monastery of Optina, to consult a famous spiritual director, Father Ambrose, to whom both Gogol and Tolstoy had confessed. Father Ambrose is the model for Father Zossima in *The Brothers Karamazov*.

At Optina Dostoevsky also met Soloviev, whose *Twelve Lectures on Godmanhood* are said to have influenced profoundly his portrayal of Christ in *The Grand Inquisitor*, while Soloviev himself is depicted in Alyosha, the youngest of the Karamazov brothers. Dostoevsky and Tolstoy both had attended the twelve lectures of Soloviev concerning Godmanhood. On Dostoevsky's return to Moscow, he predicted that he would die within two years, and he did. In June 1880 he made a valedictory speech at the unveiling of the Pushkin memorial in Moscow and received a tremendous ovation. One of the things he said was, "To be a real Russian, to be wholly Russian, means only this: to be a brother to all men, and to be universally human." When Dostoevsky died, on 28 January 1881, of a cerebral hemorrhage, vast crowds gave him "the funeral of a king."

By many he is regarded as the world's greatest novelist. Maurice Baring, a Catholic, wrote, "Supposing the Gospel of St. John were annihilated and lost to us forever; although nothing would replace it, Dostoevsky's work would more nearly replace it than any other book written by any other man." And Sigmund Freud, the Jewish founder of the psychoanalytic method, wrote that *"The Brothers Karamazov* is the most magnificent novel ever written, and the story of the Grand Inquisitor is one of the peaks in the literature of the world. It can hardly be overpraised."

The Brothers Karamazov, like two other of the greatest works of fiction, Sophocles' *Oedipus Rex* and Shakespeare's *Hamlet,* is the story of a parricide. Dmitri, Ivan, Alyosha, and their half-brother, the epileptic valet Smerdyakov, are the children of Fyodor Pavlovich Karamazov, senile, mean, and sensual. All his children, except Alyosha, who is a novice in the monastery and has found in the *staretz* Father Zossima a real father, hate old Karamazov, but for different reasons. Dmitri is in love with the same woman as his father; Ivan hates his father because he so nearly resembles him; Smerdyakov loathes him for corrupting his mother and for keeping him a serf. All three want the old man's money. When he is mysteriously murdered, all are guilty, although it is

Smerdyakov who has actually committed the crime.

Dostoevsky has given to each one of the four sons a part of himself: to Dmitri his sincerity, generosity, and courage; to Ivan his intellectual temptations and pride, his unmentionable secret sins; to Smerdyakov his malady. To the father he gave his own name; and Alyosha is both the innocent child he once was, and the saint he would become. Also, Alyosha is something more. At the novel's end, Alyosha "half laughing, half enthusiastically" tells a group of boys gathered for a funeral, " . . . we shall all rise again, certainly we shall see each other and tell each other with joy and gladness all that has happened." Alyosha, then, is also the genius, the writer in Dostoevsky, the narrator who "tells all that has happened."

It is Ivan who is the most completely articulated of all the characters, and the one in whom Dostoevsky has expressed himself most fully; it is Ivan who tells Alyosha the story of *The Grand Inquisitor*. This, he explains, is a "fantasy," a "poem," although unwritten and in prose.

Ivan has been describing to Alyosha, in sadistic detail, the sufferings of innocent children: the little girl of seven whom her father enjoys beating; the girl of five dirtied by both her parents; the boy of eight torn to pieces by the dogs of a general who deliberately sets them on the child. The agony of these children proves to Ivan's "Euclidian" mind the utter absurdity of the divinely created order of things, according to which "eternal harmony" will be established only after suffering has been inflicted on the defenseless little victims of human brutality. Ivan refuses to accept this "fabric of human destiny," wants no share in it, and therefore "most respectfully returns Him the ticket." Not even Christ who, as Alyosha points out, has suffered "for all and everything," can make Ivan change his mind. Ivan's answer to Alyosha is *The Grand Inquisitor*.

What is its meaning?

At the first, most obvious level, the story sets the person of Christ against the church founded by him. In particular, the story is an attack upon the Roman Catholic Church—not an attack on "the whole of Rome," as Alyosha points out, but on the Grand Inquisitors in its hierarchy. Be it noted, however, that, in the eyes of Ivan, the Grand Inquisitor is right, and Christ is wrong; for it is Christ whose unrealistic dreams about freedom block "universal happiness" and perpetuate a social order which a rationalistic, "Euclidian" mind cannot accept. If read within the framework of *The Brothers Karamazov*, *The Grand Inquisitor* is therefore an attack upon the Catholic Church only to those who sympathize with Alyosha, to whom Dostoevsky has given his faith. To those, however, who sympathize with Ivan, the Grand Inquisitor and his theories ought to be what they once were for Dostoevsky: the great temptation of their lives.

Dostoevsky's own faith derives its strength from the fact that he has himself passed through atheism and come out the other side. Commenting on the critics of *The Brothers Karamazov*, he wrote contemptuously, "The dolts have ridiculed my obscurantism and the reactionary character of my faith. These fools could not even conceive so strong a denial of God as the one to which I gave expression. . . The whole book is an answer to that. . . . You might search Europe in vain for so powerful an expression of atheism. Thus it is not like a child that I believe in Christ and confess Him. My hosanna has come forth from the crucible of doubt."

Dostoevsky had come to this faith in Siberia. On his way to the labor camp, a lady visiting the convicts gave him a tiny volume, the Gospels, the only book permitted by the prison authorities. From that time on, God was for Dostoevsky "not somewhere, but everywhere"; and as for the painter Cézanne "light was the hero of every picture," so, for Dostoevsky, God was the hero of every novel as well as of every life.

On another level, *The Grand Inquisitor* is a terrifying

prophecy of the totalitarian state which threatens to reduce the scope of human happiness to the happiness of "babes," united "in one unanimous and harmonious antheap."

The Grand Inquisitor promises man, as Satan promised Christ in the desert, everything in exchange for the one thing that makes man man: freedom, this terrible, absolute freedom of man's will to choose or to reject at any and every moment what his own conscience shows him to be a moral good. Wearied by this continual, uninterrupted, and inescapable act of choice which alone makes possible both the act of "free love" and the anti-social act of injustice, the Grand Inquisitor has set out to establish "universal happiness"—in the name of Christ, as he tells his followers, for the sake of "positive Christianity," as the Nazis proclaimed in their program.

It is in analyzing the three temptations of Christ that Dostoevsky shows himself at his psychological and at his theological best.

The banner of earthly bread, which is the first temptation, the banner which Christ refused to raise, is raised by all modern philosophies. "Feed men, and then ask of them virtue! that's what they'll write on the banner which they will raise against Thee," says the Grand Inquisitor; and so they have from Marx and Mazzini to Hitler, Mussolini and Stalin. But "freedom and bread enough for all are," in the opinion of the Grand Inquisitor, "inconceivable together." As long, therefore, as men are free not to choose what is best for society, a stable, perfect social order with bread enough for all is impossible.

True, man is hungry not for bread alone. He is capable by nature of searching for an object worthy of worship. But he who gives the bread can easily be mistaken for the "Lord and Giver of Life" (the English word "lord" actually comes from "hlafweard," meaning "he who guards the loaf") and so may easily become *ersatz* for the "Lord" and satisfy the "craving for community of worship" still left in the masses.

Christ refused to establish social justice by sacrificing freedom for bread. "Thou didst reject," accuses the Grand Inquisitor, "the one infallible banner which was offered Thee to make all men bow down to Thee alone— the banner of earthly bread; and Thou has rejected it for the sake of freedom and the bread of heaven."

The analysis of the second temptation—Christ refused to throw himself down from the pinnacle of the temple in order to prove that he was the Son of God— leads Dostoevsky into the problem of the "free conscience."

Man, says the Grand Inquisitor, desires "not only to live, but to have something to live for." However, this "stable object" of an other-directed life must, according to Christ's teaching, be chosen by man's free conscience, aware of good and evil and always able to choose between them. Such a choice causes "spiritual agony"; and therefore, "man prefers peace, and even death, to freedom of choice in the knowledge of good and evil." It would be better, maintains the Grand Inquisitor, better for the good of the individual and for the good of society, for man to barter his freedom of choice for "miracle, mystery, and authority."

In emphasizing that the second temptation offered Christ by the devil was to do magic, to work miracles, to offer man a search for the miraculous instead of for the holy, Dostoevsky laid his finger on one of the perennial dangers to which Christians are always subject. Dostoevsky's Grand Inquisitor sees that once man thinks himself capable of lifting himself to God, of arriving, by techniques of asceticism or prayer, at having power over God Himself, he is "in the bag" and lost. So the Grand Inquisitor suggests to Christ that man can take what he must wait to be given; and this is antichrist indeed, for Christ is God become man, never man jacked up by himself to God: God lifts man up in history, and for Dostoevsky history is just that, the lifting up by Christ on the Cross of the whole man.

The third temptation, which resulted in Christ's refusal to accept from Satan the kingdom of the world, is used by Dostoevsky to analyze man's "craving for universal unity," "the third and last anguish of men." Christ, by refusing to take "the sword of Caesar" from the hand of Satan, preferred centuries of "the confusion of free thought" to a stable society. It is time, therefore, that men like the Grand Inquisitor begin to "plan the universal happiness of man."

And this third temptation, the will to unity, the conviction that what is believed by many, or by all, is true, is a terrifying prefiguration of modern democracy. "Thou hast only Thine elect," taunts the Grand Inquisitor, "while we give rest to all." "We promise that only when they renounce their freedom and submit to us will they be free,' says the Grand Inquisitor, and defies Christ to contradict him. And when the end shall come, and Christ will call the Grand Inquisitor to account, the latter warns Him he will be not a whit abashed. "I will stand up and point out to Thee the thousand millions of happy children who have known no sin." But on earth, since the Fall, man cannot safely be unaware of what he does; the only safely ignorant people are children. The artificially protracted childishness, by which the masses have no idea that in abandoning their freedom of choice they are abandoning their capacity to know or choose good from evil, is total guilt. True that those who abandon their freedom of choice to the Grand Inquisitor can no longer sin, since the Grand Inquisitor sins for them, but they have, in giving up their freedom, placed themselves outside of God's providence. The Gestapo officers who only obeyed orders are the perfect examples of how truly Dostoevsky prophesied. The sinner so long as he knows he sins is in his place in creation; the person who has "most respectfully returned Him the ticket" is marginal, powerless thereafter to turn toward God or away from Him. To know we sin is the first step in faith and toward forgiveness.

Dostoevsky's Christ, that is, the Christ who rejected the devil's offer, and who is the prisoner of the Grand Inquisitor, does not show himself as the Incarnate Word, who assumed in His flesh and blood the eternal travail of the Father, and answered Pilate's "Art Thou a King?" with the proud "Thou sayest it" of the Gospel. Dostoevsky's Christ remains silent, and His only answer is to kiss the Grand Inquisitor on the lips.

What is the meaning of this kiss?

The only man who kissed Christ in the Gospels was Judas. Is Christ's kiss in Ivan's story analogous? Reminiscent? Is it approval?

Or is it the Divine pardon? "For if our heart condemn us, God is greater than our heart and knoweth all things," St. John wrote (I John iii, 20). Dostoevsky does not tell; he leaves us an enigma, and since he leaves us with a question let us agree that "we know all the answers; it is the questions that we do not know."

There have been many conjectures as to where Dostoevsky got the idea for *The Grand Inquisitor*. It is quite possible that Dostoevsky found his theme among the *Carmina Burana,* a collection of ribald parodies by the wandering scholars, or Goliardes, of the Middle Ages, who wandered from town to town living on their wits and their songs. Published in 1847, one of these parodies, the "Gospel according to the Mark of Silver," describes how "the Pope said to the Romans: 'When the Son of Man shall come to the seat of Our Majesty, say you first to him "Friend, for what comest Thou?" And if He shall persevere in refusing to give you anything, cast Him into outer darkness.' Then it came to pass that a certain Poor Clerk came to the court of our Lord Pope and cried out, saying, 'Have pity on me, because poverty has me in thrall. For indeed I am miserable and poor, therefore I pray you come to the aid of my calamity and have mercy on me.' But those hearing Him waxed indignant and said, 'Friend, may your poverty accompany you to perdition. Get Thee behind us, Satan, for Thou dost not know the things that are of Mammon.' "

Other suggestions are that he took some part of the Grand Inquisitor's character from Victor Hugo's Torquemada, or from the Grand Inquisitor in Friedrich Schiller's *Don Carlos*. In this latter, the Grand Inquisitor and the King's confessor, the scoundrel Domingo, are contrasted with a Carthusian prior.

Whatever the spark may be that ignited this story, it is one that will burn on as long as there are human beings on earth to read it.

The translation used is the familiar one by Constance Garnett.

A.F.

SELECTED BIBLIOGRAPHY

Berdjajew, Nicolai. *Die Weltanschauung Dostojewskijs.* München, 1925.

Chulkov, J. *How Dostoevski Wrote.* Moscow, 1939.

de Lubac, Henri. *The Drama of Atheist Humanism.* New York, 1950.

Dostoyevsky, Fyodor. *The Brothers Karamazov.* New York, The Modern Library.

Evdokimoff, P. *Dostoevski et le pouvoir du mal.* Paris, 1942.

Guardini, Romano. *Religiöse Gestalten in Dostojewskijs Werk.* München, 1947.

Iswolsky, Helene. *The Great Books: A Christian Appraisal.* New York, 1953

Maceina, Antanas. *Der Grossinquisitor.* Heidelberg, 1952.

Szylkarski, Wladimir. *Solowjew und Dostojewskij.* Bonn, 1948.

Troyat, Henry. *Dostoevski.* Paris, 1940.

Zouboff, Peter P. *Vladimir Solovjev on Godmanhood.* New York, International Universities Press.

THE GRAND INQUISITOR

" . . . Do you know, Alyosha—don't laugh! I made a poem about a year ago. If you can waste another ten minutes on me, I'll tell it to you."

"You wrote a poem?"

"Oh, no, I didn't write it," laughed Ivan, "and I've never written two lines of poetry in my life. But I made up this poem in prose and I remembered it. I was carried away when I made it up. You will be my first reader—that is, listener. Why should an author forego even one listener?" smiled Ivan. "Shall I tell it to you?"

"I am all attention," said Alyosha.

"My poem is called 'The Grand Inquisitor'; it's a ridiculous thing, but I want to tell it to you.". . .

"My story is laid in Spain, in Seville, in the most terrible time of the Inquisition, when fires were lighted every day to the glory of God, and 'in the splendid *auto da fé* the wicked heretics were burnt.' . . .

"In His infinite mercy He came once more among men in that human shape in which He walked among men for three years fifteen centuries ago. He came down to the 'hot pavement' of the southern town in which on the day before almost a hundred heretics had, *ad majorem gloriam Dei,* been burnt by the cardinal, the Grand Inquisitor, in a magnificent *auto da fé,* in the presence of the king, the court, the knights, the cardinals, the most charming ladies of the court, and the whole population of Seville.

"He came softly, unobserved, and yet, strange to say, every one recognized Him. That might be one of the best passages in the poem. I mean, why they recognized Him. The people are irresistibly drawn to Him, they surround Him, they flock about Him, follow Him. He moves silently in their midst with a gentle smile of infinite compassion. The sun of love burns in His heart, light and power shine from His eyes, and their radiance, shed on the people, stirs their hearts with responsive love. He holds out His hands to them, blesses them, and a healing virtue comes from contact with Him, even with His garments. And old man in the crowd, blind from childhood, cries out, 'O Lord, heal me and I shall see Thee!' and, as it were, scales fall from his eyes and the blind man sees Him. The crowd weeps and kisses the earth under His feet. Children throw flowers before Him, sing, and cry hosannah. 'It is He— it is He!' all repeat. 'It must be He, it can be no one but Him!' He stops at the steps of the Seville cathedral at the moment when the weeping mourners are bringing in a little open white coffin. In it lies a child of seven, the only daughter of a prominent citizen. The dead child lies hidden in flowers. 'He will raise your child,' the crowd shouts to the weeping mother. The priest, coming to meet the coffin, looks perplexed, and frowns, but the mother of the dead child throws herself at His feet with a wail. 'If it is Thou, raise my child!' she cries, holding out her hands to Him. The procession halts, the coffin is laid on the steps at His feet. He looks with compassion, and His lips once more softly pronounce, 'Maiden, arise!' and the maiden arises. The little girl sits up in the coffin and looks round, smiling with wide-open wondering eyes, holding a bunch of white roses they had put in her hand.

"There are cries, sobs, confusion among the people, and at that moment the cardinal himself, the Grand Inquisitor, passes by the cathedral. He is an old man, almost ninety, tall and erect, with a withered face and sunken eyes, in which there is still a gleam of light. He is not dressed in his gorgeous cardinal's robes, as he was the day before, when he was burning the enemies of the Ro-

2

man Church—at that moment he was wearing his coarse, old, monk's cassock. At a distance behind him come his gloomy assistants and slaves and the 'holy guard.' He stops at the sight of the crowd and watches it from a distance. He sees everything; he sees them set the coffin down at His feet, sees the child rise up, and his face darkens. He knits his thick grey brows and his eyes gleam with a sinister fire. He holds out his finger and bids the guards take Him. And such is his power, so completely are the people cowed into submission and trembling obedience to him, that the crowd immediately makes way for the guards, and in the midst of deathlike silence they lay hands on Him and lead Him away. The crowd instantly bows down to the earth, like one man, before the old inquisitor. He blesses the people in silence and passes on.

"The guards lead their prisoner to the close, gloomy vaulted prison in the ancient palace of the Holy Inquisition and shut Him in it. The day passes and is followed by the dark, burning 'breathless' night of Seville. The air is 'fragrant with laurel and lemon.' In the pitch darkness the iron door of the prison is suddenly opened and the Grand Inquisitor himself comes in with a light in his hand. He is alone; the door is closed at once behind him. He stands in the doorway and for a minute or two gazes in His face. At last he goes up slowly, sets the light on the table and speaks.

The Grand Inquisitor speaks to the prisoner " 'Is it Thou? Thou?' but receiving no answer, he adds at once, 'Don't answer, be silent. What canst Thou say, indeed? I know too well what Thou wouldst say. And Thou hast no right to add anything to what Thou hadst said of old. Why, then, art Thou come to hinder us? For Thou hast come to hinder us, and Thou knowest that. But dost Thou know what will be tomorrow? I know not who Thou art and care not to know whether it is Thou or only a semblance of Him, but tomorrow I shall condemn Thee and burn Thee at the stake as the worst of heretics. And the very people who have today kissed Thy feet, tomorrow at the faintest sign from me will rush to heap up the embers of Thy fire. Knowest Thou that? Yes, maybe Thou knowest it,' he added with thoughtful penetration, never for a moment taking his eyes off the Prisoner.''

"I don't quite understand, Ivan. What does it mean?'' Alyosha, who had been listening in silence, said with a smile. "Is it simply a wild fantasy, or a mistake on the part of the old man—some impossible *qui pro quo*?''

"Take it as the last,'' said Ivan, laughing, "if you are so corrupted by modern realism and can't stand anything fantastic. If you like it to be a case of mistaken identity, let it be so. It is true,'' he went on, laughing, "the old man was ninety, and he might well be crazy over his set idea. He might have been struck by the appearance of the Prisoner. It might, in fact, be simply his ravings, the delusion of an old man of ninety, overexcited by the *auto da fé* of a hundred heretics the day before. But does it matter to us after all whether it was a mistake of identity or a wild fantasy? All that matters is that the old man should speak out, should speak openly of what he has thought in silence for ninety years.''

"And the Prisoner too is silent? Does He look at him and not say a word?''

"That's inevitable in any case,'' Ivan laughed again. "The old man has told Him He hasn't the right to add anything to what He has said of old. One may say it is the most fundamental feature of Roman Catholicism, in my opinion at least. 'All has been given by Thee to the Pope,' they say 'and all, therefore, is still in the Pope's hands, and there is no need for Thee to come now at all. Thou must not meddle for the time, at least.' That's how they speak and write too—the Jesuits, at any rate. I have read it myself in the works of their theologians.''

4

" 'Hast Thou the right to reveal to us one of the mysteries of that world from which Thou hast come?' my old man asks Him, and answers the question for Him. 'No, Thou hast not; that Thou mayest not add to what has been said of old, and mayest not take from men the freedom which Thou didst exalt when Thou wast on earth. Whatsoever Thou revealest anew will encroach on men's freedom of faith; for it will be manifest as a miracle, and the freedom of their faith was dearer to Thee than anything in those days fifteen hundred years ago. Didst Thou not often say then, "I will make you free"? But now Thou hast seen these "free" men,' the old man adds suddenly, with a pensive smile. 'Yes, we've paid dearly for it,' he goes on, looking sternly at Him, 'but at last we have completed that work in Thy name. For fifteen centuries we have been wrestling with Thy freedom, but now it is ended and over for good. Dost Thou not believe that it's over for good? Thou lookest meekly at me and deignest not even to be wroth with me. But let me tell Thee that now, today, people are more persuaded than ever that they have perfect freedom, yet they have brought their freedom to us and laid it humbly at our feet. But that has been our doing. Was this what Thou didst? Was this Thy freedom?' "

"I don't understand again," Alyosha broke in. "Is he ironical, is he jesting?"

"Not a bit of it! He claims it as a merit for himself and his Church that at last they have vanquished freedom and have done so to make men happy."

" 'For now' (he is speaking of the Inquisition, of course) 'for the first time it has become possible to think of the happiness of men. Man was created a rebel; and how can rebels be happy? Thou wast warned,' he says to Him. 'Thou hast had no lack of admonitions, and warnings, but Thou didst not listen to those warnings; Thou didst reject the only way by which men might be made happy. But, fortunately, departing Thou didst hand on the work to us. Thou hast promised, Thou hast established by Thy word, Thou hast given to us the right to bind and to unbind, and now, of course, Thou canst not think of taking it away. Why, then, hast Thou come to hinder us?' "

"And what's the meaning of 'no lack of admonitions and warnings'?" asked Alyosha.

"Why, that's the chief part of what the old man must say."

The three temptations fore-shadowed the whole subsequent history of mankind " 'The wise and dread Spirit, the spirit of self-destruction and non-existence,' the old man goes on, 'the great spirit talked with Thee in the wilderness, and we are told in the books that he "tempted" Thee. Is that so? And could anything truer be said than what he revealed to Thee in three questions and what Thou didst reject, and what in the books is called "the temptation"? And yet if there has ever been on earth a real stupendous miracle, it took place on that day, on the day of the three temptations. The statement of those three questions was itself the miracle. If it were possible to imagine simply for the sake of argument that those three questions of the dread spirit had perished utterly from the books, and that we had to restore them and to invent them anew, and to do so had gathered together all the wise men of the earth—rulers, chief priests, learned men, philosophers, poets—and had set them the task to invent three questions, such as would not only fit the occasion, but express in three words, three human phrases, the whole future history of the world and of humanity—dost Thou believe that all the wisdom of the earth united could have invented anything in depth and force equal to the three questions which were actually put to Thee then by the wise and mighty spirit in the wilderness? From those questions alone, from the miracle of their statements, we can see that we have here to do not with the fleeting human intelligence, but with the absolute and eternal. For in those three questions the whole subsequent history of mankind is, as it were, brought together into one whole, and foretold, and in them are united all the unsolved historical contradictions of human nature. At the time it could not be so clear, since the future was unknown; but now that fifteen hundred years have passed, we see that everything in those three questions was so justly divined and foretold, and has been so truly fulfilled, that nothing can be added to them or taken from them.

The first temptation: the problem of bread. " 'Judge Thyself who was right—Thou or he who questioned Thee then? Remember the first question; its meaning, in other words, was this: "Thou wouldst go into the world, and art going with empty hands, with some promise of freedom which men in their simplicity and their natural unruliness cannot even understand, which they fear and dread — for nothing has ever been more insupportable for a man and a human society than freedom. But seest Thou these stones in this parched and barren wilderness? Turn them into bread, and mankind will run after Thee like a flock of sheep, grateful and obedient, though for ever trembling, lest Thou withdraw Thy hand and deny them Thy bread." But Thou wouldst not deprive man of freedom and didst reject the offer, thinking, what is that freedom worth, if obedience is bought with bread? Thou didst reply that man lives not by bread alone. But dost Thou know that for the sake of that earthly bread the spirit of the earth will rise up against Thee and will strive with Thee and overcome Thee, and all will follow him, crying, "Who can compare with this beast? He has given us fire from heaven!" Dost Thou know that the ages will pass, and humanity will proclaim by the lips of their sages that there is no crime, and therefore no sin; there is only hunger? "Feed men, and then ask of them virtue!" that's what they'll write on the banner, which they will raise against Thee, and with which they will destroy Thy temple. Where Thy temple stood will rise a new building; the terrible tower of Babel will be built again, and though, like the one of old, it will not be finished, yet Thou mightest have prevented that new tower and have cut short the sufferings of men for a thousand years; for they will come back to us after a thousand years of agony with their tower. They will seek us again, hidden underground in the catacombs, for we shall be again persecuted and tortured. They will find us and cry to us, "Feed us, for those who have promised us fire from heaven haven't given it!" And then we shall finish building their tower, for he finishes the building who feeds them. And we alone shall feed them in Thy name, declaring falsely that it is in Thy name. Oh, never, never can they feed themselves without us! No science will give them bread so long as they remain free. In the end they will lay their freedom at our feet, and say to us, "Make us your slaves, but feed us." They will understand themselves, at last, that freedom and bread enough for all are inconceivable together, for never, never will they be able to share between them! They will be convinced, too, that they can never be free, for they are weak, vicious, worthless and rebellious.

" 'Thou didst promise them the bread of Heaven, but, I repeat again, can it compare with earthly bread in the eyes of the weak, ever sinful and ignoble race of man? And if for the sake of the bread of Heaven thousands and tens of thousands shall follow Thee, what is to become of the millions and tens of thousands of millions of creatures who will not have the strength to forego the earthly bread for the sake of the heavenly? Or dost Thou care only for the tens of thousands of the great and strong, while the millions, numerous as the sands of the sea, who

8

are weak but love Thee, must exist only for the sake o the great and strong? No, we care for the weak too. They are sinful and rebellious, but in the end they too will become obedient. They will marvel at us and look on us as gods, because we are ready to endure the freedom which they have found so dreadful to rule over them—so awful it will seem to them to be free. But we shall tell them that we are Thy servants and rule them in Thy name. We shall deceive them again, for we will not let Thee come to us again. That deception will be our suffering, for we shall be forced to lie.

" 'This is the significance of the first question in the wilderness, and this is what Thou hast rejected for the sake of that freedom which Thou hast exalted above everything. Yet in this question lies hid the great secret of this world.

" 'Choosing "bread," Thou wouldst have satisfied the universal and everlasting craving and humanity—to find some one to worship.

" 'So long as man remains free he strives for nothing so incessantly and so painfully as to find some one to worship. But man seeks to worship what is established beyond dispute, so that all men would agree at once to worship it. For these pitiful creatures are concerned not only to find what one or the other can worship, but to find something that all would believe in and worship; what is essential is that all may be *together* in it. This craving for *community* of worship is the chief misery of every man individually and of all humanity from the beginning of time. For the sake of common worship they've slain each other with the sword. They have set up gods and challenged one another, "Put away your gods and come and worship ours, or we will kill you and your gods!" And so it will be to the end of the world, even when gods disappear from the earth; they will fall down before idols just the same. Thou didst know, Thou couldst not but have known, this fundamental secret of human nature, but Thou didst reject the one infallible banner which was offered Thee to make all men bow down to Thee alone— the banner of earthly bread; and Thou hast rejected it for the sake of freedom and the bread of Heaven.

The second temptation: the problem of conscience.

" 'Behold what Thou didst further. And all again in the name of freedom! I tell Thee that man is tormented by no greater anxiety than to find some one quickly to whom he can hand over that gift of freedom with which the ill-fated creature is born. But only one who can appease their conscience can take over their freedom. In bread there was offered Thee an invincible banner; give bread, and man will worship Thee, for nothing is more certain than bread. But if some one else gains possession of his conscience—oh! then he will cast away Thy bread and follow after him who has ensnared his conscience. In that Thou wast right. For the secret of man's being is not only to live but to have something to live for. Without a stable conception of the object of life, man would not consent to go on living, and would rather destroy himself than remain on earth, though he had bread in abundance. That is true.

" 'But what happened?

" 'Instead of taking men's freedom from them, Thou didst make it greater than ever! Didst Thou forget that man prefers peace, and even death, to freedom of choice in the knowledge of good and evil? Nothing is more seductive for man than his freedom of conscience, but nothing is a greater cause of suffering. And behold, instead of giving a firm foundation for setting the conscience of man at rest for ever, Thou didst choose all that is exceptional, vague and enigmatic; Thou didst choose what was utterly beyond the strength of men, acting as though Thou didst not love them at all—Thou who didst come to give Thy life for them! Instead of taking possession of men's freedom, Thou didst increase it, and burdened the spiritual kingdom of mankind with its sufferings for ever. Thou

10

didst desire man's free love, that he should follow Thee freely, enticed and taken captive by Thee. In place of the rigid ancient law, man must hereafter with free heart decide for himself what is good and what is evil, having only Thy image before him as his guide. But didst Thou not know he would at last reject even Thy image and Thy truth, if he is weighed down with the fearful burden of free choice? They will cry aloud at last that the truth is not in Thee, for they could not have been left in greater confusion and suffering than Thou hast caused, laying upon them so many cares and unanswerable problems.

" 'So that, in truth, Thou didst Thyself lay the foundation for the destruction of Thy kingdom, and no one is more to blame for it. Yet what was offered Thee? There are three powers, three powers alone, able to conquer and to hold captive for ever the conscience of these impotent rebels for their happiness—those forces are miracle, mystery and authority. Thou hast rejected all three and hast set the example for doing so. When the wise and dread spirit set Thee on the pinnacle of the temple and said to Thee, "If Thou wouldst know whether Thou art the Son of God then cast Thyself down, for it is written: the angels shall hold him up lest he fall and bruise himself, and Thou shalt know then whether Thou art the Son of God and shalt prove then how great is Thy faith in Thy father." But Thou didst refuse and wouldst not cast Thyself down. Oh! of course, Thou didst proudly and well like God; but the weak, unruly race of men, are they gods? Oh, Thou didst know then that in taking one step, in making one movement to cast Thyself down, Thou wouldst be tempting God and have lost all Thy faith in Him, and wouldst have been dashed to pieces against that earth which Thou didst come to save. And the wise spirit that tempted Thee would have rejoiced. But I ask again, are there many like Thee? And couldst Thou believe for one moment that men, too, could face such a temptation?

Is the nature of men such, that they can reject miracle, and at the great moments of their life, the moments of their deepest, most agonizing spiritual difficulties, cling only to the free verdict of the heart?

" 'Oh, Thou didst know that Thy deed would be recorded in books, would be handed down to remote times and the utmost ends of the earth, and Thou didst hope that man, following Thee, would cling to God and not ask for a miracle. But Thou didst not know that when man rejects miracle he rejects God too; for man seeks not so much God as the miraculous. And as man cannot bear to be without the miraculous, he will create new miracles of his own for himself, and will worship deeds of sorcery and witchcraft, though he might be a hundred times over a rebel, heretic, and infidel. Thou didst not come down from the Cross when they shouted to Thee, mocking and reviling Thee, "Come down from the cross and we will believe that Thou art He." Thou didst not come down, for again Thou wouldst not enslave man by a miracle, and didst crave faith given freely, not based on miracle. Thou didst crave for free love and not the base raptures of the slave before the might that has overawed him for ever.

" 'But Thou didst think too highly of men therein, for they are slaves, of course, though rebellious by nature. Look around and judge; fifteen centuries have passed, look upon them. Whom hast Thou raised up to Thyself? I swear, man is weaker and baser by nature than Thou hast believed him! Can he, can he do what Thou didst? By showing him so much respect, Thou didst, as it were, cease to feel for him, for Thou didst ask far too much from him—Thou who hast loved him more than Thyself! Respecting him less, Thou wouldst have asked less of him. That would have been more like love, for his burden would have been lighter. He is weak and vile. What though he is everywhere now rebelling against our power, and proud of his rebellion? It is the pride of a child and a schoolboy. They are little children rioting and barring out the teacher at school. But their childish delight will end; it will cost them dear. They will cast down temples and drench the earth with blood. But they will see at last, the foolish children, that, though they are rebels, they are impotent rebels, unable to keep up their own rebellion. Bathed in their foolish tears, they will recognize at last that He who created them rebels must have meant to mock at them. They will say this in despair, and their utterance will be a blasphemy which will make them more unhappy still, for man's nature cannot bear blasphemy, and in the end always avenges it on itself. And so unrest, confusion and unhappiness—that is the present lot of man after Thou didst bear so much for their freedom!

" 'Thy great prophet tells in vision and in image, that he saw all those who took part in the first resurrection and that there were of each tribe twelve thousand. But if there were so many of them, they must have been not men but gods. They had borne Thy cross, they had endured scores of years in the barren, hungry wilderness, living upon locusts and roots—and Thou mayest indeed point with pride at those children of freedom, of free love, of free and splendid sacrifice for Thy name. But remember that they were only some thousands; and what of the rest? And how are the other weak ones to blame, because they could not endure what the strong have endured? How is the weak soul to blame that it is unable to receive such terrible gifts? Canst Thou have simply come to the elect and for the elect? But if so, it is a mystery and we cannot understand it. And if it is a mystery, we too have a right to preach a mystery, and to teach them that it's not the free judgment of their hearts, not love that matters, but a mystery which they must follow blindly, even against their conscience. So we have done. We have corrected Thy work and have founded it upon *miracle, mystery* and *authority*. And men rejoiced that they were again led like sheep, and that the terrible gift that had brought them such suffering, was, at last, lifted from their hearts.

" 'Were we right teaching them this?

" 'Speak!

" 'Did we not love mankind, so meekly acknowledging their feebleness, lovingly lightening their burden, and permitting their weak nature even sin with our sanction? Why hast Thou come now to hinder us? And why dost Thou look silently and searchingly at me with Thy mild eyes? Be angry. I don't want Thy love, for I love Thee not. And what use is it for me to hide anything from Thee? Don't I know to Whom I am speaking? All that I can say is known to Thee already. And is it for me to conceal from Thee our mystery? Perhaps it is Thy will to hear it from my lips.

The third temptation: the problem of unity.

" 'Listen, then. We are not working with Thee, but with *him*—that is our mystery. It's long—eight centuries—since we have been on *his* side and not on Thine. Just eight centuries ago, we took from him what Thou didst reject with scorn, that last gift he offered Thee, showing Thee all the kingdoms of the earth. We took from him Rome and the sword of Caesar, and proclaimed ourselves sole rulers of the earth, though hitherto we have not been able to complete our work. But whose fault is that? Oh, the work is only beginning, but it has begun. It has long to await completion and the earth has yet much to suffer, but we shall triumph and shall be Caesars, and then we shall plan the universal happiness of man. But Thou mightest have taken even the sword of Caesar.

" 'Why didst Thou reject that last gift?

" 'Hadst Thou accepted that last counsel of the mighty spirit, Thou wouldst have accomplished all that man seeks on earth—that is, some one to worship, some one to keep his conscience, and some means of uniting all in one unanimous and harmonious antheap, for the craving for universal unity is the third and last anguish of

14

men. Mankind as a whole has always striven to organize a universal state. There have been many great nations with great histories, but the more highly they were developed the more unhappy they were, for they felt more acutely than other people the craving for worldwide union. The great conquerors, Timours and Ghenghis-Khans, whirled like hurricanes over the face of the earth striving to subdue its people, and they too were but the unconscious expression of the same craving for universal unity. Hadst Thou taken the world and Caesar's purple, Thou wouldst have founded the universal state and have given universal peace. For who can rule men if not he who holds their conscience and their bread in his hands.

" 'We have taken the sword of Caesar, and in taking it, of course, have rejected Thee and followed *him*.

" 'Oh, ages are yet to come of the confusion of free thought, of their science and cannibalism. For having begun to build their tower of Babel without us, they will end, of course, with cannibalism. But then the beast will crawl to us and lick our feet and spatter them with tears of blood. And we shall sit upon the beast and raise the cup, and on it will be written, "Mystery." But then, and only then, the reign of peace and happiness will come for men.

" 'Thou art proud of Thine elect, but Thou hast only the elect, while we give rest to all. And besides, how many of those elect, those mighty ones who could become elect, have grown weary waiting for Thee, and have transferred and will transfer the powers of their spirit and the warmth of their heart to the other camp, and end by raising their *free* banner against Thee. Thou didst Thyself lift up that banner. But with us all will be happy and will no more rebel nor destroy one another as under Thy freedom.

" 'Oh, we shall persuade them that they will only become free when they renounce their freedom to us and submit to us. And shall we be right or shall we be lying? They will be convinced that we are right, for they will remember the horrors of slavery and confusion to which Thy freedom brought them. Freedom, free thought and science, will lead them into such straits and will bring them face to face with such marvels and insoluble mysteries, that some of them, the fierce and rebellious, will destroy themselves, others, rebellious but weak, will destroy one another, while the rest, weak and unhappy, will crawl fawning to our feet and whine to us: ''Yes, you were right, you alone possess His mystery, and we come back to you, save us from ourselves!''

Summary: the Inquisitor's Utopia.

'' 'Receiving bread from us, they will see clearly that we take the bread made by their hands from them, to give it to them, without any miracle. They will see that we do not change the stones to bread, but in truth they will be more thankful for taking it from our hands than for the bread itself! For they will remember only too well that in old days, without our help, even the bread they made turned to stones in their hands, while since they have come back to us, the very stones have turned to bread in their hands. Too, too well they know the value of complete submission! And until men know that, they will be unhappy. Who is most to blame for their not knowing it, speak? Who scattered the flock and sent it astray on unknown paths? But the flock will come together again and will submit once more, and then it will be once for all. Then we shall give them the quiet humble happiness of weak creatures such as they are by nature. Oh, we shall persuade them at last not to be proud, for Thou didst lift them up and thereby taught them to be proud. We shall show them that they are weak, that they are only pitiful children, but that childlike happiness is the sweetest of all. They will become timid and will look to us and huddle close to us in fear, as chicks to the hen. They will marvel at us and will be awe-stricken before us, and will be proud at our being so powerful and clever, that we have been

16

able to subdue such a turbulent flock of thousands of millions. They will tremble impotently before our wrath, their minds will grow fearful, they will be quick to shed tears like women and children, but they will be just as ready at a sign from us to pass to laughter and rejoicing, to happy mirth and childish song. Yes, we shall set them to work, but in their leisure hours we shall make their life like a child's game, with children's songs and innocent dance. Oh, we shall allow them even sin, they are weak and helpless, and they will love us like children because we allow them to sin. We shall tell them that every sin will be expiated, if it is done with our permission, that we allow them to sin because we love them, and the punishment for these sins we take upon ourselves. And we shall take it upon ourselves, and they will adore us as their saviours who have taken on themselves their sins oefore God. And they will have no secrets from us. We shall allow or forbid them to live with their wives and mistresses, to have or not to have children—according to whether they have been obedient or disobedient—and they will submit to us gladly and cheerfully. The most painful secrets of their conscience, all, all they will bring to us, and we shall have an answer for all. And they will be glad to believe our answer, for it will save them from the great anxiety and terrible agony they endure at present in making a free decision for themselves. And all will be happy, all the millions of creatures except the hundred thousand who rule over them. For only we, we who guard the mystery, shall be unhappy.

" 'There will be thousands of millions of happy babes, and a hundred thousand sufferers who have taken upon themselves the curse of the knowledge of good and evil. Peacefully they will die, peacefully they will expire in Thy name, and beyond the grave they will find nothing but death. But we shall keep the secret, and for their happiness we shall allure them with the reward of heaven and eternity. Though if there were anything in the other world, it certainly would not be for such as they.

" 'It is prophesied that Thou wilt come again in victory, Thou wilt come with Thy chosen, the proud and strong, but we will say that they have only saved themselves, but we have saved all. We are told that the harlot who sits upon the beast, and holds in her hands the *mystery,* shall be put to shame, that the weak will rise up again, and will rend her royal purple and will strip naked her loathsome body. But then I will stand up and point out to Thee the thousand millions of happy children who have known no sin. And we who have taken their sins upon us for their happiness will stand up before Thee and say: "Judge us if Thou canst and darest." Know that I fear Thee not. Know that I too have been in the wilderness, I too have lived on roots and locusts, I too prized the freedom with which Thou hast blessed men, and I too was striving to stand among Thy elect, among the strong and powerful, thirsting "to make up the number." But I awakened and would not serve madness. I turned back and joined the ranks of those *who have corrected Thy work.* I left the proud and went back to the humble, for the happiness of the humble. What I say to Thee will come to pass, and our dominion will be built up. I repeat, tomorrow Thou shalt see that obedient flock who at a sign from me will hasten to heap up the hot cinders about the pile on which I shall burn Thee for coming to hinder us. For if any one has ever deserved our fires, it is Thou. Tomorrow I shall burn Thee. *Dixi.*' "

Ivan stopped. He was carried away as he talked and spoke with excitement; when he had finished, he suddenly smiled.

Alyosha had listened in silence; toward the end he was greatly moved and seemed several times on the point of interrupting, but restrained himself. Now his words came with a rush.

"But. . . that's absurd!" he cried, flushing. "Your

poem is in praise of Jesus, not in blame of Him—as you meant it to be. And who will believe you about freedom? Is that the way to understand it? That's not the idea of it in the Orthodox Church. . . That's Rome, and not even the whole of Rome, it's false—those are the worst of the Catholics, the Inquisitors, the Jesuits! . . .And there could not be such a fantastic creature as your Inquisitor. What are these sins of mankind they take on themselves? Who are these keepers of the mystery who have taken some curse upon themselves for the happiness of mankind? When have they been seen? We know the Jesuits, they are spoken ill of, but surely they are not what you describe? They are not that at all, not at all . . . . They are simply the Romish army for the earthly sovereignty of the world in the future, with the Pontiff of Rome for Emperor. . . that's their ideal, but there's no sort of mystery or lofty melancholy about it. . . It's simple lust of power, of filthy earthly gain, of domination—something like a universal serfdom with them as masters—that's all they stand for. They don't even believe in God perhaps. Your suffering inquisitor is a mere fantasy.''

"Stay, stay," laughed Ivan, "how hot you are! A fantasy you say, let it be so! Of course it's a fantasy. But allow me to say: do you really think that the Roman Catholic movement of the last centuries is actually nothing but the lust of power, of filthy earthly gain? Is that Father Païssy's teaching?''

"No, no, on the contrary, Father Païssy did once say something the same as you. . .but of course it's not the same, not a bit the same," Alyosha hastily corrected himself.

" A precious admission, in spite of your 'not a bit the same.' I ask you why your Jesuits and Inquisitors have united simply for vile material gain? Why can there not be among them one martyr oppressed by great sorrow and loving humanity? You see, only suppose that there was one such man among all those who desire nothing but filthy material gain — if there's only one like my old inquisitor, who had himself eaten roots in the desert and made frenzied efforts to subdue his flesh to make himself free and perfect. But yet all his life he loved humanity, and suddenly his eyes were opened, and he saw that it is no great moral blessedness to attain perfection and freedom, if at the same time one gains the conviction that billions of God's creatures have been created as a mockery, that they will never be capable of using their freedom, that these poor rebels can never turn into giants to complete the tower, that it was not for such geese that the great idealist dreamt his dream of harmony. Seeing all that he turned back and joined — the clever people. Surely that could have happened?''

"Joined whom, what clever people?" cried Alyosha, completely carried away. "They have no such great cleverness and no mysteries and secrets. . .Perhaps nothing but Atheism, that's all their secret. Your inquisitor does not believe in God, that's his secret!"

"What if it is so! At last you have guessed it. It's perfectly true that that's the whole secret, but isn't that suffering, at least for a man like that, who has wasted his whole life in the desert and yet could not shake off his incurable love of humanity? In his old age he reached the clear conviction that nothing but the advice of the great dread spirit could build up any tolerable sort of life for the feeble, unruly 'incomplete, empirical creatures created in jest.' And so, convinced of this, he sees that he must follow the council of the wise spirit, the dread spirit of death and destruction, and therefore accept lying and deception, and lead men consciously to death and destruction, and yet deceive them all the way so that they may not notice where they are being led, that the poor blind creatures may at least on the way think themselves happy. And note, the deception is in the name of Him in Whose ideal the old man had so fervently believed all his life long. Is not that tragic? And if only one such stood at the head of the whole army 'filled with the lust of power only for the sake of filthy gain' — would not one such be enough to make a tragedy? More than that, one such standing at the head is enough to create the actual leading idea of the Roman Church with all its armies and Jesuits, its highest idea. I tell you frankly that I firmly believe that there has always been such a man among those who stood at the head of the movement. Who knows, there may have been some such even among the Roman Popes. Who knows, perhaps the spirit of that accursed old man who loves mankind so obstinately in his own way, is to be found even now in a whole multitude of such old men, existing not by chance but by agreement, as a secret league formed long ago for the guarding of the mystery, to guard it from the weak and the unhappy, so as to make them happy. No doubt it is so, and so it must be indeed. I fancy that even among the Masons there's something of the same mystery at the bottom, and that that's why the Catholics so detest the Masons as their rivals breaking up the unity of the idea, while it is so essential that there should be one flock and one shepherd. . . . But from the way I defend my idea I might be an author impatient of your criticism. Enough of it.''

''You are perhaps a Mason yourself!'' broke suddenly from Alyosha. ''You don't believe in God,'' he added, speaking this time very sorrowfully. He fancied besides that his brother was looking at him ironically. ''How does your poem end?'' he asked, suddenly looking down. ''Or was it the end?''

''I meant it to end like this:

''When the Inquisitor ceased speaking he waited some time for his Prisoner to answer him. His silence weighed down upon him. He saw the Prisoner had listened intently all the time, looking gently in his face and evidently not wishing to reply. The old man longed for Him to say something, however bitter and terrible. But He suddenly approached the old man in silence and softly kissed him on his bloodless aged lips. That was all His answer. The old man shuddered. His lips moved. He went to the door, opened it, and said to Him: 'Go, and come no more. . . Come not at all, never, never!' And he let Him out into the dark alleys of the town. The Prisoner went away.''

''And the old man?''

''The kiss glows in his heart, but the old man adheres to his idea.''